There are three cats in this book. They're on the next page...

For Gwyn

First published 2014 by Walker Books Ltd,
87 Vauxhall Walk, London SE11 5HJ

This edition published 2015

6 8 10 9 7 5

Viviane Schwarz © 2014

This book has been typeset in Kingthings
Trypewriter and hand-lettered by Viviane Schwarz

Printed in Malaysia

British Library Cataloguing in Publication
Data: a catalogue record for this book is
available from the British Library

ISBN 978-1-4063-6090-5

www.walker.co.uk

WALKER BOOKS
AND SUBSIDIARIES
LONDON • BOSTON • SYDNEY • AUCKLAND

There are three cats <u>and</u> a dog in this book. They are all your friends.

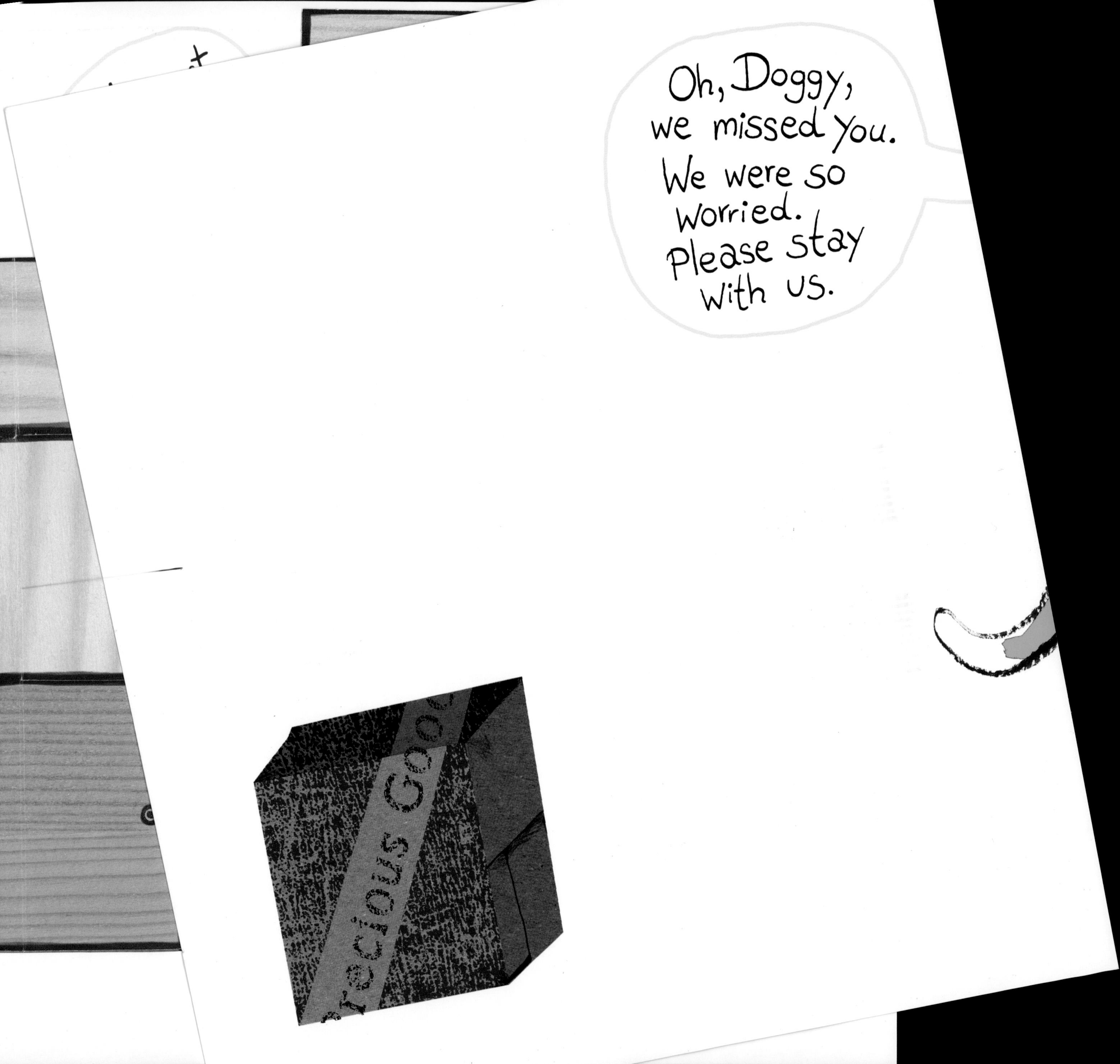
Oh, Doggy, we missed you. We were so worried. Please stay with us.

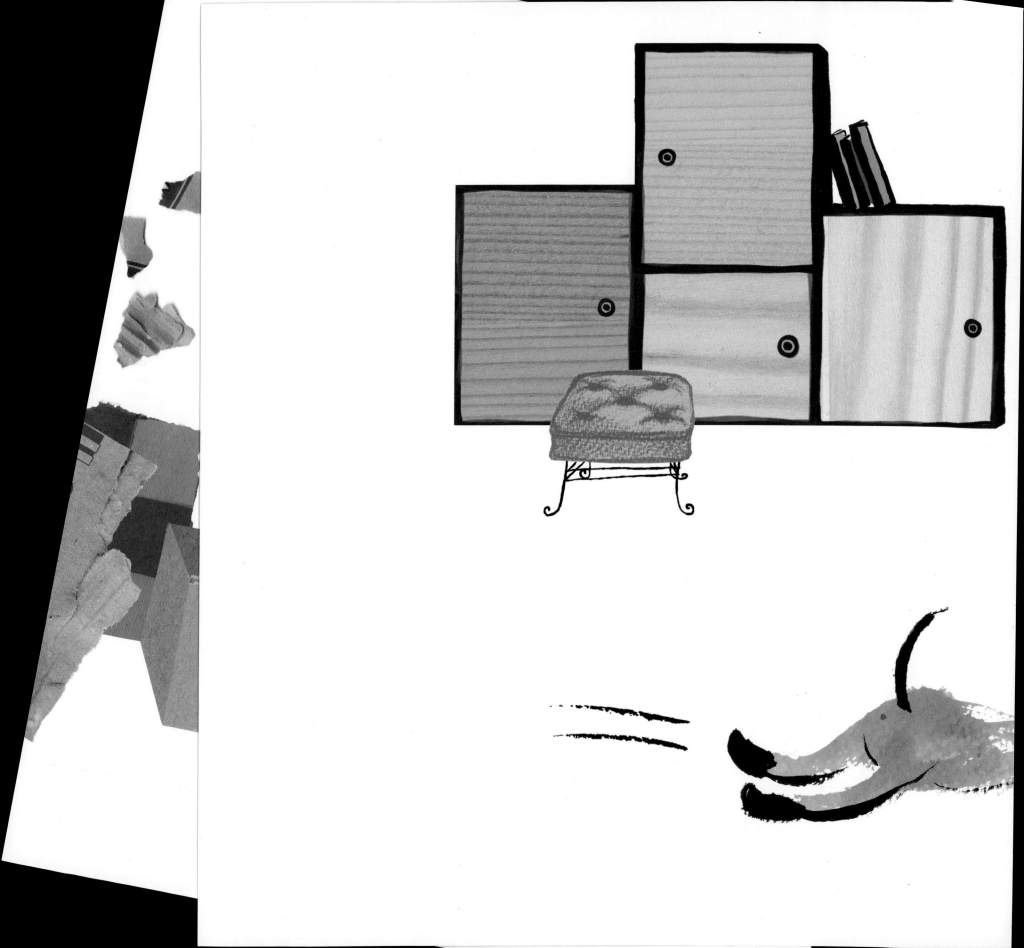

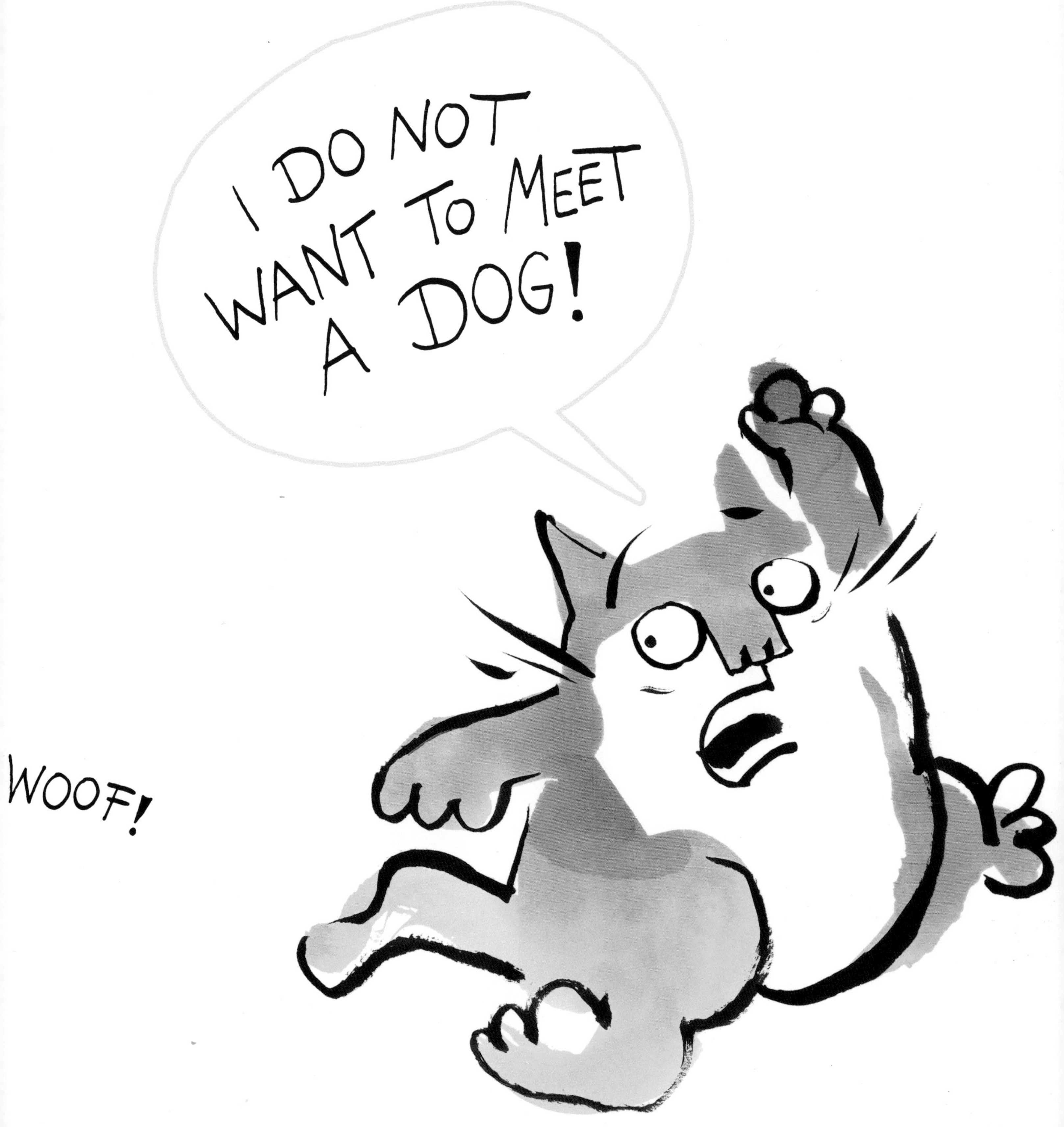
I DO NOT WANT TO MEET A DOG!
WOOF!

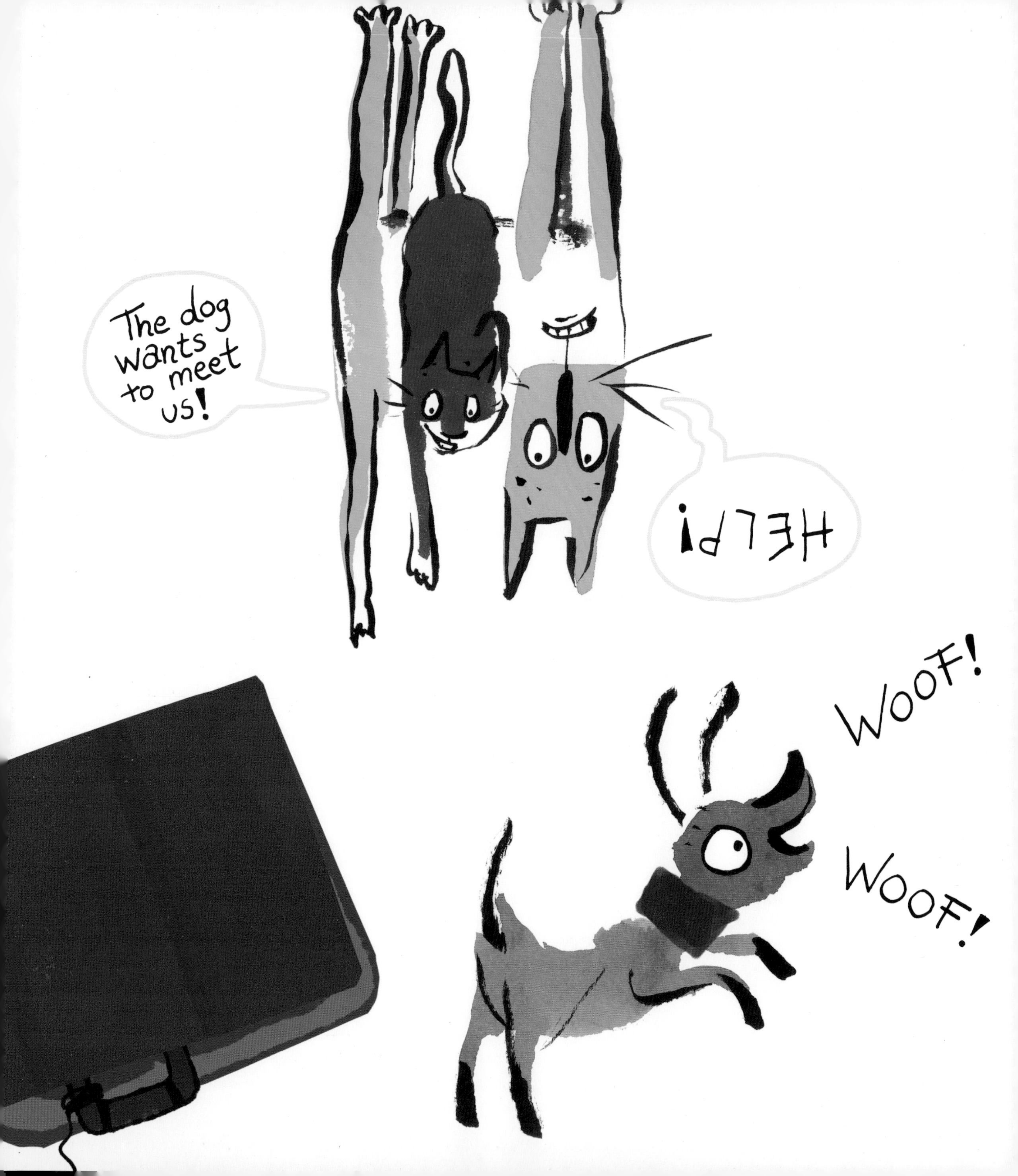
The dog wants to meet us!
HELP!
WOOF!
WOOF!

That piano was no good.
This wardrobe is much safer. Nobody open the doors this time!